Marvin, the Blue Pig

By Karen Wallace

Illustrated by Lisa Williams

Special thanks to our advisers for their expertise:

Adria F. Klein, Ph.D.
Professor Emeritus, California State University
San Bernardino, California

Susan Kesselring, M.A.
Literacy Educator
Rosemount-Apple Valley-Eagan (Minnesota) School District

PICTURE WINDOW BOOKS
Minneapolis, Minnesota

Levels for *Read-it!* Readers

- Familiar topics
- Frequently used words
- Repeating patterns

- New ideas
- Larger vocabulary
- Variety of language structures

- Challenges in ideas
- Expanded vocabulary
- Wide variety of sentences

- More complex ideas
- Extended vocabulary range
- Expanded language structures

A Note to Parents and Caregivers:

Read-it! Readers are for children who are just starting on the amazing road to reading. These beautiful books support both the acquisition of reading skills and the love of books.

The RED LEVEL presents familiar topics using common words and repeating sentence patterns.

The BLUE LEVEL presents new ideas using a larger vocabulary and varied sentence structure.

The YELLOW LEVEL presents more challenging ideas, a broad vocabulary, and wide variety in sentence structure.

The GREEN LEVEL presents more complex ideas, an extended vocabulary range, and expanded language structures.

When sharing a book with your child, read in short stretches, pausing often to talk about the pictures. Have your child turn the pages and point to the pictures and familiar words. And be sure to reread favorite stories or parts of stories.

There is no right or wrong way to share books with children. Find time to read with your child, and pass on the legacy of literacy.

Adria F. Klein, Ph.D.
Professor Emeritus
California State University
San Bernardino, California

First American edition published in 2005 by
Picture Window Books
5115 Excelsior Boulevard
Suite 232
Minneapolis, MN 55416
877-845-8392
www.picturewindowbooks.com

First published in Great Britain by Franklin Watts, 96 Leonard Street,
London, EC2A 4XD

Text © Karen Wallace 2002
Illustration © Lisa Williams 2002

Printed in the United States of America.

Library of Congress Cataloging-in-Publication Data
Wallace, Karen.
Marvin, the blue pig / by Karen Wallace ; illustrated by Lisa Williams.
p. cm. — (Read-it! readers)
Summary: The other animals on the farm make fun of Marvin because he is not pink
like the other pigs, but his attempt to change his color has surprising results.
ISBN 1-4048-0564-8 (hardcover)
[1. Pigs—Fiction. 2. Domestic animals—Fiction. 3. Color—Fiction. 4. Individuality—
Fiction.] I. Williams, Lisa, 1970- ill. II. Title. III. Series.
PZ7.W1568Mar 2004
[E]—dc22
2004007327

Marvin was a sad pig. He wasn't pink like most pigs or even spotted like some pigs.

Marvin was sad because he was a blue pig.

Marvin's best friend in the
barnyard was a spotted pig
named Esther.

Esther danced and told Marvin
jokes to try to cheer him up.

Marvin's mother was called
Mrs. Pig. She was big, pink,
and very wise.

"If you want to be pink, you have to be happy," she said to Marvin. "If you're feeling blue, then you look blue!"

One day, there was an argument
about who was the best animal in
the barnyard.

"I'm the loveliest," said the rooster.
"I'm the strongest," said the horse.

"I'm the fluffiest," said the sheep.

"And I'm the milkiest," said the cow.

11

"What are you, Marvin?" asked
Mrs. Pig. But before Marvin could
reply, the rooster jumped onto
the gate.

"He's the BLUEST!" crowed the rooster,
and all the animals laughed.

Marvin ran away and locked himself in his pigpen.

Mrs. Pig went to see Marvin.
"Son," she said with a huge sigh,
"if I've told you once, I've told you
a thousand times—if you want to
be pink, you have to be happy!"

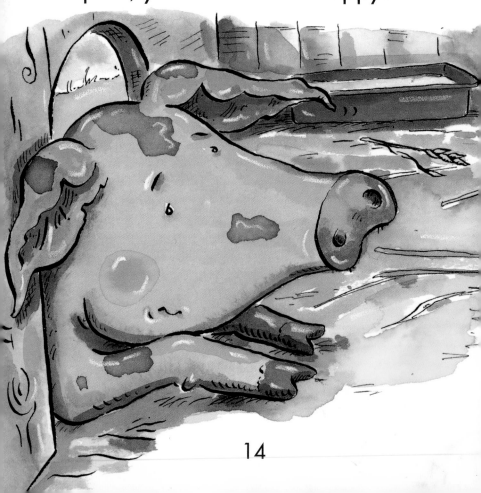

"I've tried," sniffed Marvin.

"Well, you'll just have to try
harder," replied Mrs. Pig firmly.

15

Then Esther scratched on the
pigpen door. "I know how you can
turn pink, Marvin," she whispered.

Marvin poked his head out of the
door. "How?" he asked.

"I heard the farmer talking to his children," said Esther.

"So what?" Marvin answered rudely.

"He said wonderful things would happen if they ate their vegetables," said Esther. "So why not try some?"

That night, Marvin crept into
the garden.

He wasn't sure which vegetables to
eat, so he ate a little of everything.

When Marvin woke up the next morning, something wonderful had happened.

He wasn't blue anymore!

His legs were green like lettuce.

His tail was orange like a carrot.

His back was as red as a tomato.

His tummy was purple like a
beet. And his face was as
yellow as sweet corn.

"You look amazing!" said the rooster.

"Terrific!" said the horse.

"Fabulous!" said the sheep.

"Tremendous!" said the cow.

Marvin was astonished.

None of the animals
had ever been kind to him before.

Mrs. Pig was so proud. She puffed up to twice her size and snorted like a steam train.

A brand new feeling crept over
Marvin. "I feel happy!" he cried.

And guess what?

Marvin turned pink!

Levels for *Read-it!* Readers

**Read-it!* Readers help children practice early reading
skills with brightly illustrated stories.**

Red Level: Familiar topics with frequently used words and
repeating patterns.

I Am in Charge of Me by Dana Meachen Rau
Let's Share by Dana Meachen Rau

Blue Level: New ideas with a larger vocabulary and a variety
of language structures.

At the Beach by Patricia M. Stockland
The Playground Snake by Brian Moses

Yellow Level: Challenging ideas with an expanded vocabulary
and a wide variety of sentences.

Flynn Flies High by Hilary Robinson
Marvin, the Blue Pig by Karen Wallace
Moo! by Penny Dolan
Pippin's Big Jump by Hilary Robinson
The Queen's Dragon by Anne Cassidy
Sounds Like Fun by Dana Meachen Rau
Tired of Waiting by Dana Meachen Rau
Whose Birthday Is It? by Sherryl Clark

Green Level: More complex ideas with an extended vocabulary
range and expanded language structures.

Clever Cat by Karen Wallace
Flora McQuack by Penny Dolan
Izzie's Idea by Jillian Powell
Naughty Nancy by Anne Cassidy
The Princess and the Frog by Margaret Nash
The Roly-Poly Rice Ball by Penny Dolan
Run! by Sue Ferraby
Sausages! by Anne Adeney
Stickers, Shells, and Snow Globes by Dana Meachen Rau
The Truth About Hansel and Gretel by Karina Law
Willie the Whale by Joy Oades

A complete list of *Read-it!* Readers is available on our Web site:
www.picturewindowbooks.com